This book belongs to:

....

THE UNSCARY SCARECROW

Written & Illustrated by John Patience

DERRYDALE BOOKS
New York
© Fern Hollow Productions Ltd:
Peter Haddock Ltd., U.K.
This 1984 edition is published by Derrydale Books,
distributed by Crown Publishers, Inc.
Printed in Italy
ISBN 0-517-445743

Farmer Bramble had woken up bright and early. He had a very busy day ahead of him, and as usual he and his family were enjoying a hearty breakfast.

"Cock a doodle-do, cock a doodle-do," crowed Farmer Bramble's rooster, flying up onto the kitchen window sill.

"You're late again, rooster," chuckled Farmer Bramble. "It's a good thing I've got a proper alarm clock to wake me up in the morning — you're certainly not an early riser!"

After his breakfast, feeling very happy, Farmer Bramble went out to begin his day's work. He was singing a little song —

"Fern Hollow is the place to be
The leaves are green on every tree
The sky is blue, don't need a brolly
And I'm a farmer, round and jolly."

The little song came to an abrupt end as Farmer Bramble noticed a flock of big black crows in his field, all greedily gobbling up the wheat.

"Be off with you," shouted the angry badger, rushing around the field and waving his arms about. "Leave my wheat alone!"

But the poor old farmer, being rather too fat, soon grew tired and had to stop for breath. Then the bold crows settled down again to eating his crop.

Mrs. Bramble decided that the best thing to do was to build a scarecrow. Of course, the three children were happy to help. It was all great fun. A turnip was used for the scarecrow's head and his old clothes were stuffed with hay and tied with string. He looked really marvelous. But when he was put in the field, the crows sat on his hat and arms and kept on eating the wheat. The scarecrow just wasn't very scary!

When Mr. Periwinkle, the postman, arrived with Mr. Bramble's letters, he suggested that the scarecrow might be more effective if he had a scary face.

"That's a good idea," agreed Mr. Bramble. "I've got some cans of paint and a brush. Perhaps you would like to paint the scarecrow's face on for me, Mr. Periwinkle."

The postman was an eager amateur artist, and was
really rather pleased to show off his abilities. The job only
took five minutes and everyone admitted that the face was
very scary indeed. But the bold crows took no notice of it
at all, and continued eating Farmer Bramble's wheat!

As the Brambles stood wondering what on earth they could do to get rid of the pesky crows, the Fern Hollow express passed by, and Mr. Rusty, the engine driver, gave the farmers a friendly wave and sounded the train's whistle.

Toot, toot. Toot, toot, went the train whistle loudly, and all the crows flew up into the air. The whistle had frightened them away, but soon they came back again and began, once more, to gobble up the wheat. Then Mr. Bramble rubbed his chin and smiled.

"I've got an idea," he said to his wife.

Wasting no time, Farmer Bramble drove his tractor round to the railroad station, where he went to see his friend the engine driver. Mr. Rusty was in the engine shed polishing up the brass fittings on the train.

"Hello there Farmer Bramble," he said cheerily. "What can I do for you?"

"Well, I was wondering if you had an old train whistle you could let me have," replied the badger.

"I should think so," said Mr. Rusty helpfully, fishing around in a pile of bits and pieces. "Yes, here's one."

Farmer Bramble thanked his friend profusely and
drove off on his tractor.

"I wonder what he is going to do with an old train
whistle," mumbled Mr. Rusty, scratching his head.

Back at the farm, the clever badger began building a peculiar machine. It was made up of all kinds of odd things; an alarm clock, an old car engine, bits of string, levers and pulleys, and most important of all, the engine whistle. When it was finally completed the farmer filled his machine with gas and, with the help of Tugger, carried it out into the wheat field and stood it by the side of the scarecrow. All the crows in the field stopped eating and eyed the machine suspiciously.

"Stand back everyone," cried Farmer Bramble, and he pulled hard on the starting cord.

Chug, chug, chug, went the machine, and for a while that's all it did. Then, quite suddenly, it blew the old engine whistle.

Toot, toot! Toot, toot!

It sounded just like the Fern Hollow express, and the greedy crows were so frightened that they all flew away. To make sure that the pests did not come back, Farmer Bramble had designed his machine to blow the whistle automatically every ten minutes.

"Hip hip hooray, the crows have gone away!" shouted Tugger, and everyone laughed. As for the unscary scarecrow — he never said a word!

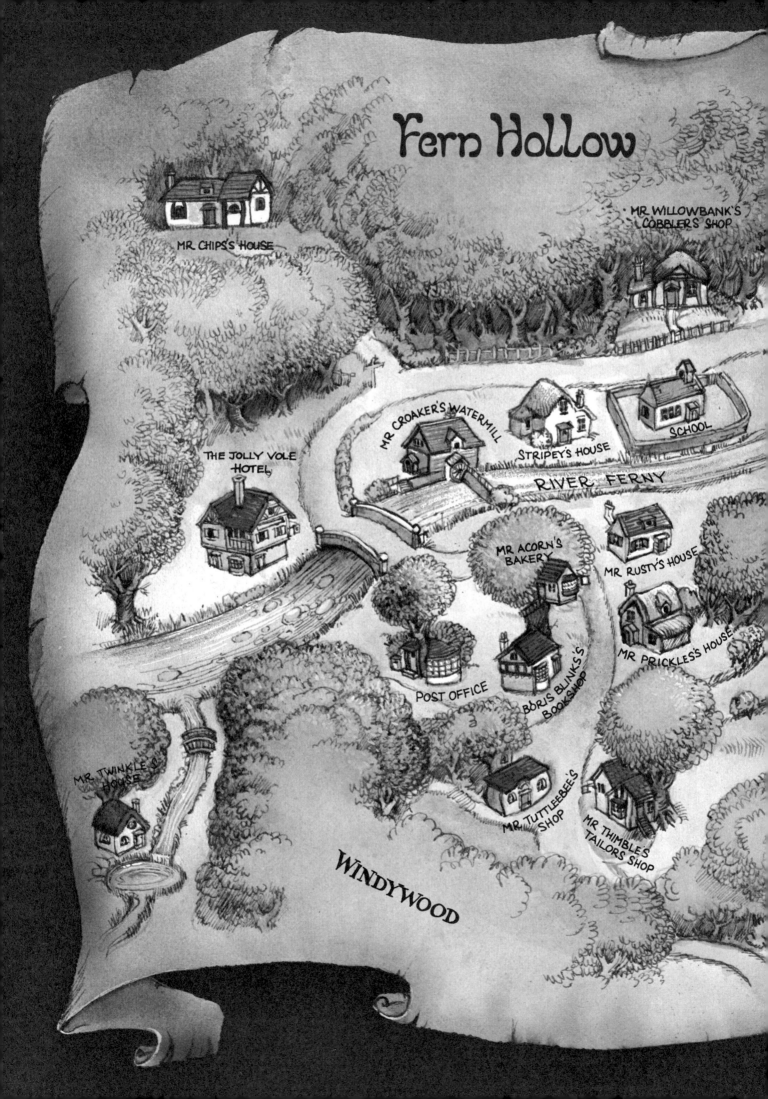